SECRET SINGER

A SHORT STORY

ALEXANDRIA BLAELOCK

BlueMere Books
MELBOURNE, AUSTRALIA

For permission requests, please contact
enquiries@bluemerebooks.com.

Ordering Information:
Discounts are available on quantity purchases. For details, contact orders@bluemerebooks.com.

Secret Singer/Alexandria Blaelock
paperback ISBN: 978-1-925749-39-7
digital ISBN: 978-1-925749-40-3

Book Layout © BookDesignTemplates.com

SECRET SINGER

Cosima avoided the old clanky lift and skipped down the long circling flight of stairs instead.

It had to be said that the elegantly imposing stairwell was one of two reasons she'd booked into the hotel in the first place.

The stairs climbed from the ground floor, round and around in marble circles to the fifth floor.

And unlike other old and once-imposing family homes converted into small boutique hotels, this one maintained the same high-quality finishes from the ground to the roof.

No slumming servants in this once prosperous household.

At least not in the main house.

As you descended the stairs (or ascended if you were that way inclined) the light from the glass light well dimmed and brightened as clouds obscured the sun.

Now and again, the light cast the silhouette of a bird against the white plastered wall.

Seeming to fly by your side, keeping you company on your long journey to wherever.

Happily, being old stairs, the engineering ensured the smell of cooking stayed beneath them. Only fresh or at least freshly air-conditioned air was sucked upwards.

With a slight hint of some kind of perfuming agent, probably the large fiery bright floral arrangement placed in the centre of a table in the centre of the open ground floor space beneath them.

And as you walked down (or up), leaning over the balustrade, the arrangement provided an incredible, if somewhat dizzying, kaleidoscopic view.

The thick, deep purple plush stair runner was stunning in its plain simplicity, secured against the stair treads with slightly tarnished chrome rods.

It went some way towards containing the echoes, but without other distractions, you could still hear the whispers of other guests waiting for the lifts.

Must have been a fun place for a bit of espionage activity in the house's heyday.

It was also the perfect place to indulge all kinds of fantasies involving tiaras, masked balls, and holiday romances.

Though circular stairs are notoriously difficult to vacuum, and the carpet was in need of a good going over.

From an artistic point of view, Cosima appreciated the variety of refuse that decorated the stairway. Including sparkling paper-lined aluminium foil chewing gum wrappers, glistening pieces of thick, clear cellophane from some kind of packaged snack, and when the sun hit it, a glowing gold coin.

Though the coin was not from a country where she was likely to spend it.

While it is perfectly possible to imagine staid middle-aged astrophysicists, molecular biologists and chemical whatsists named Cosima, our Cosima was almost exactly what you would think to look for if someone said, "hey look; there's Cosima!"

A tiny, dark-haired, imp-faced pixie. Except, perhaps, a little more plumptious, probably due to too much time spent dreaming.

Because, of course, she worked in the creative arts, and spent entirely too much time in her imagination.

As you would.

The second reason she was staying in this particular hotel was the glorious, as well as enormous mural painted in the ground floor Salon.

That the family who owned the hotel hosted free drinks for guests on a Friday night in that very Salon was an added bonus!

However.

Cosima was not actually on vacation, though she would not decline a holiday romance should one be offered.

She was, in fact, part of a gallery exchange programme - a couple of weeks doing someone else's job in Rome, while that person did hers back home in Australia.

Working holiday!

Best of both worlds.

Having arrived the day before, Cosima was headed downstairs for a spot of breakfast before heading off to her first day of work.

So very exciting.

She might be a bit jet-lagged and close to worn out, but nonetheless, it was all a big adventure.

And she happily imagined hours spent restoring artwork, and designing publicity flyers, and maybe guiding small groups of English-speaking visitors around the gallery.

Half the fun was not knowing what might happen.

And, of course, she also happily imagined the placement as a moody Fellini film, *La Dolce Vita* for example.

Which was why she'd packed a number of slim black dresses for her travel wardrobe. And suitably flat shoes for walking.

Because you just never knew what might come your way.

Breakfast was a wonderfully continental selection of bread, and cheese, and thinly sliced meats, with deliciously sweet, milky coffee.

But by the time she realised there was a selection of cakes and pastries through a side door, it was too late. She was already full of fresh, tasty mozzarella, lightly seasoned and drizzled with olive oil.

It was a short walk to her place of work, or it would have been if she hadn't boldly strode out in entirely the wrong direction and had to take a hair-raising cab ride to get there in time.

No problem. First full day in a big city on the other side of the planet.

That wasn't overflowing with native English speakers.

And sadly, her first day of work was not exactly the Roman holiday she'd been hoping for either. There was some sweeping up after the unboxing of new art, which she was not permitted to touch and barely to look at.

There was some stuffing and stamping of envelopes of promotional materials.

And some fetching and carrying for her new boss and colleagues.

Though it might have been easier had she learned a bit more Italian before she left home.

Despite being told by Vincenzo to throw herself into hamming up the accent, it wasn't quite enough to communicate effectively.

And she felt like a condescending idiot when she did.

The plate of fresh seafood pasta in a light tomato sauce she ate at a sidewalk cafe on the walk back to her hotel helped her mood a great deal.

As did the first and second cold, crisp glasses of Pinot Grigio she drank with it.

Relaxing a little to the recorded background of some kind of opera. Something vaguely familiar. Familiar enough to hum along with, perhaps *Così Fan Tutte*.

Thinking perhaps a show at the *Teatro dell'Opera di Roma* might not go amiss. A cheap seat at a matinee.

Because it was Rome, after all. And she could no more skip the opera than the Trevi Fountain, the Colleseum, or the Piazza di Spagna.

She greeted Domenico at reception on her way back in, slipped through to the bar and ordered a lovely bitter Campari.

Then took it into a little nook under the stairs to drink while she used the guest computer to check her email.

Which was a lot cheaper (free) than using her phone data (nowhere near free) for the same job.

And seeing as she was there, a couple of searches to confirm the opera at the cafe was *Così Fan Tutte*. She plugged her earbuds into the machine and listed for a while as she sipped her drink.

And as you always do, slipped down a net-rabbit hole and listened to more and more opera. A bit more Mozart, a bit of Puccini, and some Bizet.

She finished her drink, though not her emails, and the tiniest bit drunk, decided it was time for bed anyway.

Naturally, living in her imagination, she took the stairs.

Which turned out to have the perfect rise for a slow, steady and more importantly, elegant upward glide.

Most likely even in a long skirt with an extortionate sweep.

Halfway up, she heard a man singing.

In a mesmerising voice - the light, sweet freshness of a tenor, combined with the depth and drama of a baritone.

Like a slightly bitter, dark chocolate brownie.

He took her breath away.

For the duration of the song, she was spellbound.

Hand on the balustrade, one foot on one step, the other on the step above.

Eyes closed, swaying slightly in line with his dramatic interpretation.

Cosima couldn't help wondering why he was hanging out in the hotel and not singing on a stage somewhere.

But of course, competition for places in opera companies must be intense.

Because surely, everyone in Italy must sing opera.

After a moment, she realised he'd stopped singing.

As the echoes dissipated, she heard a slight scuff that suggested he was about to leave.

"Wait!" she cried.

The noise ceased, and she thought perhaps he was indeed waiting.

"Who are you?"

He chuckled, "I am no one *signorina*," he said in perfect, but lightly accented English.

As of course, he would if he worked in the hotel.

"You sing beautifully."

After a short pause, he said, "*grazie*," and with the slightest whoosh was gone.

Cosima remained where she was, unable for a moment to free herself from his spell.

Even his speaking voice resonated in her rib cage!

If he asked her nicely, she'd walk through hell for him without hesitation.

In fact, he didn't need to ask nicely, she'd probably do it anyway.

Even though she had no idea who he was or what he looked like.

A man of mystery - her Secret Singer - what's not to like?

She challenged herself to figure out who he was, even if it was the only thing she achieved before she went home.

《《 • 》》

Fabian smiled as he returned to the reception desk.

He knew who Cosima was because she'd charmed Domenico so thoroughly, he'd mentioned her several times during handover.

Domenico thought she was so sweet he wanted to swap his own, less sweet adult daughter for her.

But Fabian hadn't realised she'd taken the stairs instead of the lift when he started singing.

And once he'd realised, he felt obliged to finish the song and retreat until later.

His audition wasn't far off now, and he wanted to focus his rehearsal energy on the passages that didn't come easily to him.

In private.

If you could call the foyer of an international hotel at midnight private.

But Domenico was right, she was sweet and charming.

He cheated and looked her up in the booking system.

Here for a little over a week more.

He called up a copy of her passport page and was pleasantly surprised.

She was cute too.

And when he thought about it, he recalled seeing her at breakfast as he ate before leaving work. When he'd been busy flirting with Gabriella.

He hummed a few scales as he shuffled papers around, trying to look busy.

And after a while, he thought it might be fun to play with her a little bit.

If she was game.

And he reckoned, that if she was there the next night, then she was game.

《《 • 》》

The next day, after a selection of cakes for breakfast, Cosima greeted Domenico on her way out.

She managed to find her way to work, on foot, without getting lost.

Arriving with coffee, her new colleagues greeted her like a long-lost friend.

She enjoyed putting together a small promotional flyer.

It was a great day!

On her way back to the hotel, she stopped at a cafe with a view over the Colleseum. Savouring a plate of antipasto on the pavement, with a light, dry Lambrusco, she let the swirl of tourist conversation roll over her.

Ordinary people may have felt lonely at a table for one within a multitude. Astrophysicist Cosima may have buried her face in an academic journal and pretended she didn't mind eating alone.

But our Cosima lived in her imagination.

And at that moment, she was happy to be alone, watching the sky darken.

Because her imagination was trying to put a face on her Secret Singer.

Her location and the fluency of his singing language suggested Italian.

Though his spoken English suggested he either was or had learned from an American.

She hoped he was tall, dark and handsome.

Preferably around her age, slim and well built.

Not older, fatter, uglier.

She was fairly sure he was a hotel employee, not one of the guests, and definitely not Domenico with his raspy smoker's voice.

The singer was sufficiently at ease in his surroundings to sing out loud, taking full advantage of the acoustic conditions. It didn't seem likely a guest would sing so confidently in a strange place.

Or have such a strong operatic presentation.

Plus, he was sober, no slurring his words or losing his diaphragmatic control.

She'd heard him late at night, suggesting night staff.

From the ground floor, so perhaps reception, porter, waiter, bartender.

And at that point, imagination failed her.

She had no idea which of those jobs might make a more attractive man.

Or which might produce the better singer.

Would a porter have the largest lung capacity?

Would a waiter have better voice control?

Someone at reception would be there for the duration of their shift. If any lifting and carrying needed to be done, he'd call someone else to do it, so plenty of time to sing.

And if he was the night receptionist, he would probably only sing if he thought he was alone.

Had he waited for her to leave before singing?

Had he chosen something to sing to her in particular?

Goosebumps rose on her arms, and not just because of the cool breeze rising up the hill.

Anyway, all that kind of ruled out hanging around spying on the ground floor.

The best approach was probably to sit halfway up the stairs and wait for something to happen.

For some reason, she was very glad she'd eliminated the possibility he was a guest.

More romantic that way perhaps.

Less likely to end tragically? Or perhaps more.

A story worthy of its own operatic score.

Passing through reception, she stopped to chat to Domenico, casually discovering he was about to clock off and wishing him a good night.

And getting herself a start time in the region of 8 pm.

Nicely done, she congratulated herself, walking through to the bar.

She climbed onto a barstool and asked for a *digestivo* recommendation.

The cute Australian boy poured her a Caffo Vecchio Amaro del Capo, and they chatted for a short while about places he thought she should visit, and things she should do.

No way he was her Secret Singer mate.

She took her Amaro through to check her email, surreptitiously looking for a man who might be the singer. Though of course, the hotel staff were very discreet and invisible.

Much as she wanted to, she couldn't let herself go through to look in on reception, because that would be cheating.

Nor could she stay up any later, because it had been a long day, and she was knackered.

Besides, if yesterday was anything to go by, he wouldn't start singing until she was out of view.

In the meantime, she rummaged about in her bag for her notebook and lucky hello kitty pen. She tore a page from the book, and scrawled a note, assuming that if he spoke English, he probably could read it and maybe write it too.

Do you take requests?

C

x

She left the note on the computer keyboard and walked up the stairs again.

Slowly, watching the floor, keeping an eye on the keyboard for as long as she was able.

Which wasn't long.

And once again, when she was halfway up, he started singing from the shadows.

Unlike the night before, the tune was familiar, though she didn't know the words. Though that didn't stop her quietly humming along.

And dancing a little, up and down a couple of steps.

Pretending she was wearing a dress with a much longer and wider skirt. Wondering if there was a shop somewhere she could buy something like she was imagining.

It was wonderful.

And all too soon, the song came to an end.

She clapped and called "*bràvo.*"

"*Grazie.*"

"*Encore.*"

He snorted.

But a moment later, he started singing *That's Amore* in English. And when he reached the chorus, she sang along.

But what she lacked for in skill, she made up in enthusiasm.

And the stairway acoustics didn't hurt either.

"*Magnifica,*" he said as the echoes dissipated.

She laughed, "you flatter me."
"Never."
"Thank you," she said, "I must go now".
"*Buona Notte.*"
"You too," she said and ran up the stairs.

《《 • 》》

Fabian had been waiting for her to head upstairs.

In fact, he'd been waiting for her all day.

Every time he dozed off for a minute, she'd visited him in his dreams.

Bringing him a small glass of wine.

Pouring some pasta onto a plate.

Rubbing his feet after a hard day at work.

Kissing his head as she bustled about doing some chore or another.

Looking after their children.

Standing beside him at some red-carpet event or another.

Not bad for someone he'd never met.

He'd risked sneaking out to see the note she'd left, and wondered what kind of request she might have to make.

And due to the cant of the stairs, he'd been able to watch her dancing, knowing she thought she was unobserved.

And oh my God, she was adorable.
Could not sing to save her life
But twelve out of ten for enthusiasm.
Too adorable.
Like a puppy, only with better manners.
He grinned and pulled the cuffs of his shirt down as he returned to reception.
Looked like she wanted to play.
So what should his next move be?"

《《 • 》》

Cosima skipped down the stairs.
Partly because "hey it's Roma!" and partly because she was eager to see if her Secret Singer had answered her note.
It was where she'd left it, wedged between the keys of the computer keyboard, and for a moment, she was disappointed.
Had he not seen her note?
Had he not answered?
She took a quick look around, and finding she was alone, tiptoed over the marble floor to pick it up.
At a glance, she could see an extra line of writing, in a strong, firm hand, and folded the paper into her pocket to look at later.

She assembled a breakfast of *Bresaola* with *Caprese* salad and picked at it while she thought about his reply.

Kiss me if you can find me.

Very forward for someone she hadn't met.

Yet the idea of kissing the man she imagined was incredibly exciting.

Lord help them both if he was short and fat and ugly.

But he *sounded* young!

And confident.

And gorgeous.

And even if he was short and fat and ugly, she was out of there before too long anyway.

Even if he was tall and thin and beautiful, she was out of there.

But if he was...

Well?

Challenge accepted.

Her workday was varied and interesting, but her thoughts were with her Secret Singer.

He'd upped the stakes, so did that mean she could hang around the ground floor eavesdropping on all the male staff members?

Or would it be better to stick to her own self-imposed rules?

Or just enjoy the flirtation while it lasted, and go home with a great holiday story?

Though, stories need endings.

If she told anyone about him, they'd want to know who he was, and whether he was a good kisser.

And did they go any further, and was she going back to see him, or was he coming to her.

She could make up some nonsense, but they would that wasn't how the story was supposed to end.

Cosima was assuming he wanted her to find him.

And that he knew who she was.

But did he?

Would he reveal himself if she didn't unmask him before she left?

Would he say, "such a shame *Signorina*, we could've had so much fun. Never mind, have a good trip home, and a long and happy life".

Or was he just winding her up?

A bit of fun with the tourist to laugh about later with his friends.

But how could a man with an opera hero's voice be the villain in real life?

Driven by curiosity, she stopped at the Chinese restaurant next to the hotel for some food on her way back. And happily, she could get a simple plate of mixed dumplings to go with her rice wine.

How surprising that while they were definitely what she ordered, they were a little more Italian in flavour and style than the ones she was used to back home.

She was enjoying the last of the rice wine when she realised that she'd started listening to a conversation going on behind her.

It wasn't the words, because she didn't speak enough Italian to understand them, but there was something, aside from a Chinese accent that had snagged her attention.

Like an itch, she couldn't reach to scratch.

She looked over her shoulder and noticed a man in the dark hotel uniform at the payment counter. He had thick, dark hair, broad shoulders and slim hips.

And then her attention was stolen by the aroma of chilled coconut pudding, and she smiled at the waiter bringing it to her.

It looked delicious. She closed her eyes and savoured the flavour as she let the first semi-sweet morsel dissolve in her mouth.

And flicked them open again as she realised why the conversation had infiltrated her consciousness - the man at the counter was speaking with the Secret Singer's voice.

She'd seen the Secret Singer!

She dropped the spoon and swung around, but he was out of her view, and there was no one at the register.

He might be gone, but now she knew what the back of him looked like.

And as a dark suit wearer, he couldn't be a red-jacketed porter. She'd already disqualified the barman, so that left reception and waiters.

She picked up her spoon, and took another taste of her dessert, smiling a little as she luxuriated in the flavour.

Fully appreciating the knowledge that he was at the tall, and thin, and beautiful end of the spectrum.

So what should be her next move?

All she had to do was linger a little linger over dinner, and if he was the night receptionist, she'd see him on her way in.

And that was a very tempting thought, but she was enjoying the chase.

She finished her dessert, paid the bill and left.

Greeting Domenico on her way into the reception.

Following her usual routine, she took a drink to the guest computer. A dark, rich, thick, hot chocolate.

It might not have been the best choice, soon she was yawning, and decided to call it a night.

She unfolded the note they'd been sharing, turned it ninety degrees and added another line.

I nearly caught you today.

C

x

And wedged it once more between the keys of the keyboard.

Then slowly climbed the elegant staircase, but he did not sing before she reached her room.

She leaned over the bannister but didn't see or hear anything to suggest he was nearby.

She yawned again.

Then quietly went to bed.

But first, she made a dinner reservation at the hotel restaurant for the following night.

《《 • 》》

Fabian was distraught.

She wasn't there!

She'd gone, and he'd missed her.

Okay, maybe not distraught. Maybe more like puzzled. Perplexed.

And then he saw the note wedged into the keyboard.

He picked it out and took it back to the reception desk.

He leaned one hip against the counter as he read the note.

Where had she been that she'd seen him without her seeing him?

He'd just picked up a takeout next door...

Ah.

《《　•　》》

Cosima skipped down the stairs, straight across to the guest computer, and removed the note before heading to breakfast.

I'm sorry I missed you

Sorry he didn't see her at the restaurant?
Sorry she didn't talk to him?
Sorry he nearly got caught?
Sorry she didn't catch him?
Sorry about what exactly?
What kind of stupid message was that?
And why was she annoyed about it?
She was leaving soon anyway.
Nothing was going to come of this flirtation.
And she didn't know who he was anyway. Some nicely shaped, dark-haired man with a mesmerising voice.

She reviewed her romantic options back home; Tom from accounts, that guy she kept running into at the gym, Greg whom she'd known for 100 years.

None of them as fascinating as her Secret Singer.

She was in a bit of a mood when she left for work.

And it was the kind of mild wrongness that leached into everything she touched.

She dropped her scalding hot coffee, and not only was she in the splash zone but Signora Cardarelli the gallery executive was too. The prospect of an enormous dry-cleaning bill was not pleasant.

She glued her fingers together, and it was only the application of a strong (and highly irritating) solvent that prevented a trip to hospital to have them separated.

She lost her credit card while buying pain killers, and spent forever on the phone to her bank to cancel it and paying an enormous fee to have a replacement card expressed to the hotel.

She was tired and sore and still grumpy when she got back to the hotel. And not even a long soak in a hot bath was enough to dispel the mood.

Especially as her hand was sore and wrapped in bandages.

Though on the bright side, it was her left hand and she was right-handed.

And she'd made a reservation for dinner, so didn't need to leave the hotel.

Though she was tempted to cancel it and have room service deliver something.

Under different circumstances, she would've enjoyed it. Just a little asparagus risotto with

Pinot Grigio, followed by strawberries macerated in Moscato.

And she stayed just long enough to discover her Secret Singer was not a waiter.

The only option left was the night receptionist.

A young man Domenico described as "a bit wild."

Cosima barely knew what to think about that.

Despite preferring the lift, which was taking forever, she forced herself up the stairs.

And when she hit the usual spot, he started singing.

She paused, looked up at the ceiling above her, and then the stairs beneath her.

She was tired, and in pain, and wanted nothing more than to curl up in her own bed, with her own pillows and her dog.

Why, she wondered, was she even playing this stupid game of hide and seek with a stranger?

A stranger who was a bit wild.

Which could mean anything from liked to drink a little too much and recklessly sleep with too many women, to being some kind of mafia enforcer who left horse heads in people's beds.

A game that in such a short time had taken over her life. Rendering her barely able to breathe without thinking about him.

Some crazy guy she'd never met.

She took a deep breath and kept walking.

Fabian wondered if she was all right.

She hadn't left him a note and barely paused on her way up the stairs.

Hadn't acknowledged him in the slightest.

He was offended.

Well, maybe not offended, more like disappointed.

She was the only person who'd commented on his night time singing.

And at a loss to explain her lack of interest in continuing their game.

Aside from whatever injury her bandaged hand represented.

About the only option left to him for contact was the Friday night soiree.

Assuming she attended.

Unless...

Cosima was writing in her journal when the doorbell chimed, and she opened the door before she remembered it was a good idea to ask who was there first.

A porter held a small tray containing a glass of some kind of liqueur, a slice of dark cake, and a small, sealed packet of painkillers.

"I didn't order this," she said.

"Nonetheless, it's marked for delivery to this room."

"From who?"

"I don't know, but I expect the sender thought you would."

"I see. Well, thank you."

The porter emptied the tray onto the desk while she signed the chit, then left.

Cosima surveyed the delivery with suspicion and noticed a folded paper. She opened it and recognised the handwriting.

Feel better soon

One the one hand, a lovely surprise.

On the other, her Secret Singer definitely knew who she was.

And which room she was in.

Something else that suggested reception.

And a gift that firmed up a more positive interpretation of what "sorry I missed you" might mean.

Mmmmm! Frangelico and chocolate cake.

It was a much happier Cosima who went to bed.

《《 • 》》

Fabian watched her eat cake for breakfast, smiling slightly at the evident relish with which she ate.

Clearly feeling better this morning than the night before.

And tonight was the soiree...

《《 • 》》

Cosima enjoyed a much better day at work.

Her colleagues were sympathetic, Signora Cardarelli brushed aside her offers to pay for the cleaning, and the *Farmacia* called to say they'd found her card.

Not that it mattered; she'd already cancelled it, but it was still an amazing stroke of luck.

And she knew tonight was the night her Secret Singer would be revealed.

Though what would happen next was something she didn't even want to imagine.

Because no matter what it was, she was still leaving in a few days.

If the outcome was positive, she'd room to manoeuvre on her visa, and vacation days owing to her.

Though should she extend her visit, and should they spend more time together, it would just make leaving that much harder.

Not quite the sword of Damocles, but a bittersweet situation.

Cosima reminded herself not to get ahead of herself.

He might not even be there.

That did not prevent her buying a new dress on her way back to the hotel.

Nor did it stop her getting her hair washed, trimmed and styled.

Or getting a manicure, or buying a new lipstick.

She paid particular attention to her grooming - shaving her legs, applying her makeup more carefully than normal, and adding a spritz of duty-free perfume.

And paced up and down the landing so as not to be the first one arriving at the Salon.

As she walked slowly down the stairs, the long, full skirt of her new, floral silk dress caressed her clean-shaven legs. The sharp ends of her fresh cut hair scratched her shoulders.

Nearing the bottom, she could hear the slight murmur of conversation and clink of glasses, and smell something rich and savoury.

As she entered the Salon, she accepted a glass of a rich and complex flavoured Aglianico from the Australian barman, nodding her thanks as she took her first sip.

She heard a conversation in English and headed over to join the table, listening to the discussion of sites to see, and things to do. Making mental notes on what to follow up.

And as her glass lowered, she watched the waiters circulate the room, trying to pick her Secret Singer. But they were too tall, or short, or thin, or fat.

She was beginning to feel like Goldilocks.

Until his voice came from behind her, *"Signorina?"*

She paused for a moment, and closed her eyes, nervous about what she might see.

And then she opened them and turned to meet his green eyes.

He was beautiful.

Square jaw, clean-shaven, slight smile.

Smelling citrusy clean and fresh.

He topped up her glass, then moved to top up the others at the table, and onto the next table.

They were limited by the fact of his being at work.

So Cosima contented herself by moving her chair slightly to watch him.

He circulated the room, chatted with guests, waited at the bar, talked with his colleagues.

Now and again, he looked at her and smiled slightly.

She couldn't help but smile back, as she imagined marriage, children, grandchildren with him.

An entire lifetime, even though they hadn't really spoken, and didn't know each other.

She watched him make another round, allowed him to top up her glass.

And watched the guests start to leave.

She watched him collect used glasses, join the other waiters in tidying the room, and disappear through a door with the empties.

And then she sat alone with what was left of her drink.

Wondering what came next.

Fabian watched her.

She was so still, she could almost be a statue.

He'd made arrangements to take the night off, so he could take her to a club or something. But she looked so elegant, self-contained and unattainable, he was afraid to ask.

Then again, she seemed to be waiting for him.

And if he didn't ask, he'd never know.

He loosened his tie.

She sighed.

Then drained her glass, stood up, and glanced around the room.

Was she looking for him?

Whatever.

He pushed himself through the door before he could change his mind.

She turned and looked at him.

And smiled.

He smiled and walked towards her, "would you care to go out for something to eat?"

Cosima smiled.

It had been an amazing trip.

She'd extended her stay, Fabian had taken some time off work, and he'd taken her to see some extraordinary sites. The ones she'd hoped to see, but hadn't expected to; Pompeii, Capri, the Amalfi Coast, and Tuscany.

They'd eaten delicious food, drunk fine wines, and tumbled into bed together.

But the spark just wasn't there.

It was such a shame.

He hugged her and kissed her forehead as he let her go, "when you come back, give me a call."

"I will," though they both knew it wasn't likely.

"And when you come to Australia, look me up."

"I will," though they both knew that was even less likely.

"I'm sorry—" he said, and at the same time she said, "it's a shame—"

And they both laughed.

"Why don't we meet up in a decade?" Fabian asked.

"Where do you suggest?"

"Somewhere neither of us have been."

They rattled through countries and cities, and Cosima suggested Tokyo.

Fabian did a quick internet search on his phone and suggested a hotel.

They agreed a date and added it to the calendars in their phones.

"Marry me if you don't find anyone else in the meantime," he said.

She made a non-committal noise, "marry me if *you* don't find anyone else in the meantime."

They laughed again.

"I'll hold you to it," he said.

"I hope so."

She turned and walked towards the departure lounge, looking back at him and waving before walking through the doors.

An amazing trip that had her questioning whether there needed to be a spark.

Or whether you could build a satisfying relationship on friendship.

《《 • 》》

Fabian watched her leave and felt the light of the day dim around him.

He'd miss her.

His phone cheeped, and he took it out to read the text

miss you already

He wondered what the Visa situation was in Australia.

miss you more

he replied.

THE END

ABOUT THE AUTHOR

Alexandria Blaelock writes stories, some of them for *Ellery Queen's Mystery Magazine* and *Pulphouse Fiction Magazine*. She's also written four self-help books applying business techniques to personal matters like getting dressed, cleaning house, and feeding your friends.

As a recovering Project Manager, she's probably too fond of sticking to plan. She lives in a forest because she enjoys birdsong, the scent of gum leaves and the sun on her face. When not telecommuting to parallel universes from her Melbourne based imagination, she watches K-dramas, talks to animals, and drinks Campari. At the same time.

Discover more at www.alexandriablaelock.com.

BOOKS BY ALEXANDRIA BLAELOCK

FICTION

That Love Nonsense

MS BLAELOCK'S BOOKS

Stress Free Dinner Parties
Signature Wardrobe Planning
Holistic Personal Finance
Minimally Viable Housekeeping

www.ingramcontent.com/pod-product-compliance
Lightning Source LLC
Chambersburg PA
CBHW070454170726
48291CB00005B/1754